God

MW00978118

# God
# Made Us

By Mrs. James Swartzentruber

Pictures by Daniel Zook and Lester Miller

## To the Teacher:

This book is designed to give constructive reading practice to pupils using the grade one *Bible Nurture and Reader Series.* It uses words that have been introduced in the reader or can be mastered with phonics skills taught by Unit 3, Lesson 25. A few new words also appear in the story, printed in italics. At the end of the book, these words are listed with pronunciations and / or illustrations to help the children to learn them on their own. Be sure the children understand that the words are vocabulary or sound words except the words in italics, and where to look to learn the new words if they need help. They should be able to read this book independently.

Books in this series with their placement according to reading and phonics lessons:

*Copyright, 1976*

By

**Rod and Staff Publishers, Inc.**

**Crockett, Kentucky 41413**

**Telephone (606) 522-4348**

Printed in U.S.A.

ISBN 978-07399-0061-1

Catalog no. 2253

14   15   16   17   18   —   21   20   19   18   17   16   15   14   13   12

Neal was playing in the grass with his tractor. He played that he was baling hay just as Father did. He had a Ford tractor just like Father's.

Father called from the house, "Come, Neal," he said. "We want

to go to *Uncle* Lukes."

Neal stood up. "Oh, good," he said. "I like to play with Lester and Seth."

He took his toys into the

house and put them away.

Then he went to wash his hands and face. He wanted to be clean. He got some soap and water. He tried to rub all the dirt off.

Then he looked to see if his face was clean. There were still some little brown spots on his face. He got some more soap and scrubbed his face really hard.

Then he looked again. His face was red because he had rubbed so hard, but he could still see the little brown spots.

He wiped his face and hands. Now he would need to change his clothes. Mother had laid out a clean shirt and clean pants for him.

When Mother saw Neal she said, "You look nice and clean, Neal."

"She does not see those little brown spots," Neal *thought*. "So they must not look too bad. I hope Lester and Seth will not see them."

Soon Neal was jumping out of the car at *Uncle* Luke's house. He forgot all about the brown spots.

"Hi, Neal," said Lester and Seth. "What would you like to play? How about a good swing? We'll push you first."

Neal liked to swing. Lester and Seth had a big swing in the large pine tree.

Neal liked to go up, up, up. He liked to swing really *high* and hit the leaves of the oak tree beside the pine, with his toes.

Then he would go down, down, and then up again.

After Neal had a ride, Lester

took a turn. Then Lester and Neal pushed Seth.

"Let's see if we can find Snowball's family," said Lester. The three boys raced to the barn. They looked and looked in the huge stack of hay.

"Let's look farther up there," said Seth, pointing to the very top of the hay.

At last they found Snowball. She had a big family. There were one, two, three, four, five little kittens in her family. Two kittens were gray striped. Two were black and white. One kitten was all white.

"I know why you call the mother cat Snowball," said Neal. "She is a white cat. I think she is pretty. She does not have one spot on her, does she?"

Then Neal looked at Lester. He did not have spots on his face. Did Seth? He looked at Seth. Seth did not have spots on his face.

"Let's go in," said Lester. "It is getting dark."

"Anyway," Seth said, "I do not think we should stay here very long. Snowball does not like to have us near her kittens."

"Maybe she will move them to another place," said Lester as they left the barn. "She does not want us to know where her family is."

When the boys came back to the house, Father and Mother were walking to the car. "Just in time, Neal," said Father with a smile when he saw him. "I was just going to call you."

"Good-bye, Lester. Good-bye, Seth," said Neal as he got into the car. "Thank you for the nice time."

Neal forgot about the brown spots on his face that night. As soon as they got home, Mother told him that it was bedtime.

But the next day, Neal remembered. He remembered about the brown spots on his face.

He looked to see if they were still there. Yes, they were. "I think I must have hundreds of brown spots. Lester and Seth do

not have brown spots as I do."

Neal tried and tried to wash the brown spots off, but they would not come off. Maybe Father could tell him how to get the brown spots off.

Neal went to see what Father was doing. He was working in the

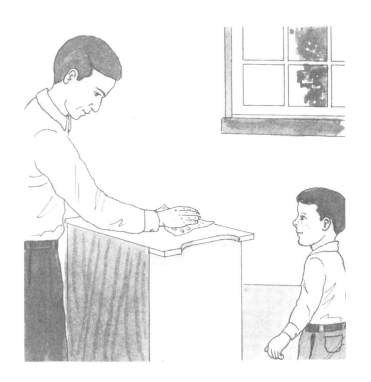

shop. He was making a *bookcase* for Mother. It was not quite finished.

Neal watched Father make the *bookcase.* Soon it was done. But it had some dirty spots on it.

Father wanted it to be nice

and clean. He got some *paper* that was all bumpy. The little bumpy spots were like sand. It was *sandpaper*.

Father rubbed the dirty spots with the *sandpaper*. The spots came off. Now the *bookcase* looked nice. It did not have any dirty spots on it anymore.

Father laid the *sandpaper* down. He took the *bookcase* into the house. He wanted to give it to Mother.

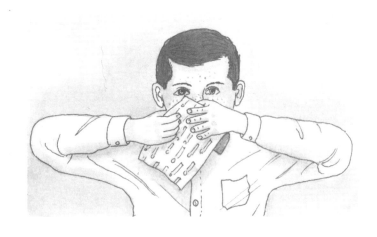

Neal looked at the *sandpaper* that Father had used. He rubbed his hands on it. He liked to feel it.

"Father used this *paper* to take the spots off the wood. Maybe this would take the little brown spots off my face, too."

There were lots of brown spots on his nose. Neal rubbed the *sandpaper* on his nose.

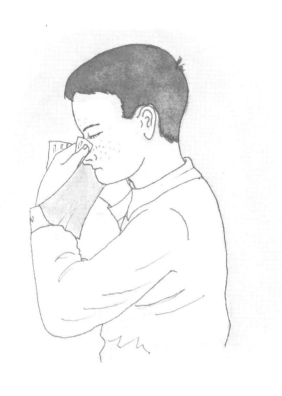

The *sandpaper* hurt. But Neal did not want brown spots on his face; so he kept rubbing.

Soon he laid the *sandpaper*

down. He ran into the house to see if the brown spots were still on his face.

He looked. Yes, they were still there. His face looked red where the *sandpaper* had scratched it. He must rub harder if he wanted to get those spots off.

Neal ran out to the shop again. He picked up the *sandpaper* and rubbed the brown spots on his face again. Oh! That hurt!

Just then Father came in. He saw what Neal was doing with the *sandpaper*. "Why are you

rubbing your face with that *sandpaper*?" asked Father.

"I want to get the brown spots off," said Neal. "This made the spots come off the *bookcase*."

"Well, well," said Father. "So it did. But *sandpaper* will not

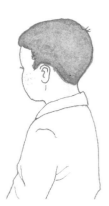

make the brown spots come off your face."

"Why?" asked Neal.

"You see," Father said, "God made those little brown spots on your face.

"Those spots are not dirt. That is just the way your skin is. You do not want to take them off if God put them there, do you?"

Neal smiled. "No," he said.

"When I was a little boy, I had brown spots on my face, too," said Father.

"I did not know that," said Neal. "Did you like them?"

"No." Father smiled. "I did not. But my father told me that God made me that way because He wanted me that way, and everything God makes is good. After that I did not mind if I had little brown spots on my face."

"I want to be like God made me, too," said Neal. "I will stop trying to take off those little brown spots." He gave the *sandpaper* to Father and ran off to play.

high (hī)

Uncle (Ung·kl)

thought (thôt)

bookcase (book·kās)

paper (pā·pėr)

sandpaper (sand·pā·pėr)